This book belongs to

From episodes of the animated TV series *Franklin*, produced by Nelvana Limited, Neurones France s.a.r.l. and Neurones Luxembourg S.A., based on the Franklin books by Paulette Bourgeois and Brenda Clark.

Franklin

Franklin is a trademark of Kids Can Press Ltd.
The character Franklin was created by Paulette Bourgeois and Brenda Clark.

The Franklin Annual: Volume 2
© 2003 Contextx Inc. and Brenda Clark Illustrator Inc.

This book includes the following stories first published in 2001:
Franklin and the Babysitter
Franklin Plants a Tree
Franklin's Birthday Party
Franklin Runs Away

All text © 2001 Contextx Inc.
All illustrations © 2001 Brenda Clark Illustrator Inc.

Franklin and the Babysitter TV tie-in adaptation written by Sharon Jennings. Illustrated by Mark Koren, Alice Sinkner, Jelena Sisic and Shelley Southern. Based on the TV episode *Franklin and the Babysitter*, written by Nicola Barton.

Franklin Plants a Tree TV tie-in adaptation written by Sharon Jennings. Illustrated by Sean Jeffrey, Mark Koren and Jelena Sisic. Based on the TV episode *Franklin Plants a Tree*, written by Brian Lasenby.

Franklin's Birthday Party TV tie-in adaptation written by Sharon Jennings. Illustrated by Sean Jeffrey, Mark Koren and Jelena Sisic. Based on the TV episode *Franklin's Birthday Party*, written by Frank Diteljan.

Franklin Runs Away TV tie-in adaptation written by Sharon Jennings. Illustrated by Sean Jeffrey, Mark Koren, Joanne Rice and Jelena Sisic. Based on the TV episode *Franklin Runs Away*, written by Bonnie Chung.

Kids Can Press acknowledges the financial support of the Ontario Arts Council, the Canada Council for the Arts and the Government of Canada, through the BPIDP, for our publishing activity.

Published in Canada by
Kids Can Press Ltd.
29 Birch Avenue
Toronto, ON M4V 1E2

Published in the U.S. by
Kids Can Press Ltd.
2250 Military Road
Tonawanda, NY 14150

www.kidscanpress.com

Series Editor: Tara Walker
Edited by Yvette Ghione
Designed by Stacie Bowes and Céleste Gagnon

Printed in China

This book is smyth sewn casebound.

CM 03 0 9 8 7 6 5 4 3 2 1

ISBN 1-55337-531-9

Kids Can Press is a *l'©rus*™ Entertainment company

The
Franklin
Annual

Kids Can Press

Contents

Franklin Plants a Tree

FRANKLIN could climb trees and swing from branches. He liked to play with his friends at the tree house and go for walks with his family in the woods. So Franklin was excited when he learned that Mr. Heron was giving away trees for Earth Day. He could hardly wait to have his own tree in his own backyard.

On Earth Day, Franklin got up early and dug a huge hole right outside his bedroom window. He wanted to plant his tree as soon as he got it home. Tonight, he'd invite his friends over to build a new tree house. Tomorrow, he'd look for an old tire and make a swing.

Franklin grabbed his wagon and hurried off. He didn't want all the big trees to be taken.

In the park, a large crowd was lined up in front of
Mr. Heron. Franklin saw lots of boxes, but he didn't
see the trees.

Maybe they're not here yet, he thought. Then he
saw Rabbit leaving.

"Don't you want a tree?" Franklin asked.
"I have one," Rabbit replied, tapping his knapsack.
Franklin was confused.

Rabbit reached into his knapsack and pulled out a tiny tree.

"That's not a tree!" Franklin exclaimed. "That's a twig."

"It's a *baby* tree, Franklin," explained Beaver. "It's called a sapling. Mine's an ash and Rabbit has an oak."

"Well, I'm not getting a sapling," Franklin declared. "My tree has to be big enough to play in *today*."

But when Franklin got to the front of the line,
Mr. Heron gave him a sapling the same size as the others.

"Could I have something bigger?" asked Franklin.

"This is a sugar maple," replied Mr. Heron. "Many
years from now it will be very big indeed."

Franklin nodded sadly. He put the sapling in his
wagon and walked slowly home.

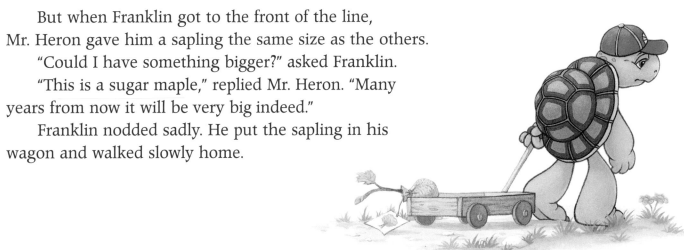

Franklin sighed as he stared at the huge hole in his backyard. He shovelled earth back in until the hole was small. Then he went to get his sugar maple.

But the sapling wasn't there.

Franklin looked all around the garden and up and down the laneway.

It must have fallen out on the way home, he decided.

At lunchtime, Franklin told his parents about losing his tree.

"But it doesn't matter," he added. "It wasn't big enough to play in."

"Big or little, you promised to care for it," said his father.

Franklin slumped down in his chair.
"All right," he sighed. "I'll go look again."

Franklin followed the path back to the park.

By the pond, he saw Beaver. Her sapling was tied to a big stick marked with notches.

"It's a growth chart," Beaver explained. "In three years, my tree will be taller than me!"

Hmmm, thought Franklin. He began to look a little harder.

In the meadow, Franklin saw Rabbit with a watering can.

"I've planted my sapling where it can get lots of fresh air and sunshine," explained Rabbit. "And I'm going to water it every day," he added.

Franklin thought about his sugar maple. If it didn't get sunshine and fresh air and water, it would never be taller than him.

Franklin started to hurry.

Near the woods, Franklin saw Bear painting a small fence bright red. Inside it was Bear's sapling.

"This will protect my pine tree until it's big and strong," Bear explained. "I don't want anyone to step on it by mistake."

Franklin thought about someone stepping on his sugar maple. If that happened, it would never grow big and strong and be taller than him.

16

Franklin told Bear everything.

"I've looked all over," Franklin moaned. "Now what do I do?"

"Maybe someone found your tree and gave it back to Mr. Heron," Bear suggested.

Franklin cheered up and ran off to find Mr. Heron.

Back at the park, Franklin saw Mr. Heron packing up boxes.

"How's your sapling doing in its new home?" Mr. Heron asked.

"I lost my tree, Mr. Heron," Franklin replied. "I've looked everywhere, but I can't find it."

Mr. Heron reached into a box and lifted out a sapling.

"Is this it, Franklin?" he asked. "Someone found it on the path."

"My tree!" cried Franklin. "Thank you, Mr. Heron! I'm going to plant it right away."

Mr. Heron smiled.

18

Before Franklin left, Mr. Heron showed him a photograph.

"That's me when I was your age," he explained, "planting my first tree."

"Did it grow?" Franklin asked.

"It sure did," Mr. Heron laughed. "We're standing under it."

Franklin looked way, way up.

"You planted the tree house tree?!" he exclaimed. Then Franklin looked down at his sapling.

"Hmmm," he said thoughtfully.

Franklin hurried home, his sapling held safely in his arms. He planted it and watered it and then he checked on it every day. And, every day, Franklin was sure that his tree grew a little taller and a little stronger.

Just like Franklin.

Activities

Word Scramble

Fill in the blanks by unscrambling the letters in each box.

1. When he goes to get his tree, Franklin brings his
   __ __ __ __ __ . | g n o a w |

2. Mr. Heron gives Franklin a sugar __ __ __ __ __ .
   | l e p m a |

3. Franklin wants a tree big enough for a
   __ __ __ __ __ . | n w i g s |

4. To measure how tall her tree grows, Beaver makes a
   growth __ __ __ __ __ . | r t a c h |

5. Bear makes a fence to protect his tree and paints it bright
   __ __ __ . | e d r |

6. The tree house tree was planted by Mr. __ __ __ __ __ .
   | n o r H e |

Tree Maze

Franklin has lost his tree. Can you help him find it?

START

FINISH

Ashley

Word Search

Franklin can't wait for his tree to grow. In the puzzle below, circle words from the story. You'll find the words going up, down, across and diagonally.

```
A T C M F R M H B K
K R T U P L A N T A
U E S W D E P J N D
S E G U R J L R F W
G Y Q E N E E G B I
R B T H N S C Z E H
O A M I B R H K O T
W V P X I S A I L R
E I U H A E V Y N A
Q J C T A L L B W E
```

ASH   PLANT
EARTH   SUNSHINE
GROW   WATER
MAPLE   TREE
PINE   TALL

Spot the Difference

Circle the picture in each row that is different from the others.

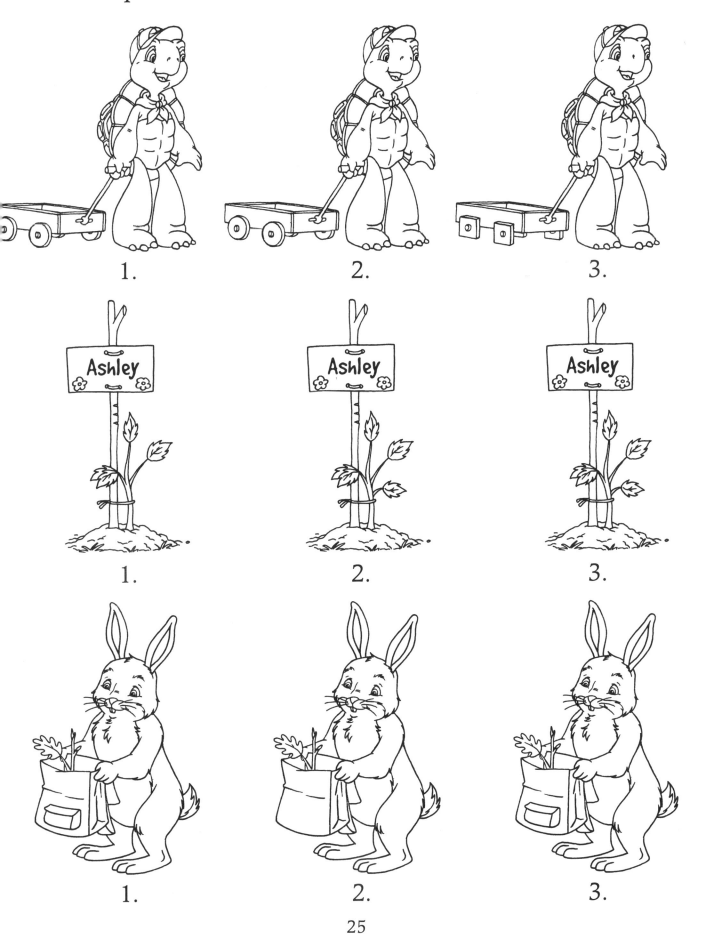

1.   2.   3.

1.   2.   3.

1.   2.   3.

Franklin's Birthday Party

FRANKLIN could count by twos and tie his shoes. He knew the days of the week and the months of the year. Soon it would be his birthday. Franklin was counting the days to the best birthday party ever.

Franklin looked at the photos in the family album.

"Last year I had a treasure hunt for my birthday," he said. "And the year before that I had a costume party."

"What do you want to do this year?" asked his mother.

"I'm not sure," replied Franklin. "But it's going to be the best party ever."

The next day, Franklin invited all of his friends to his birthday.

"What are we doing at your party?" asked Bear.

"I don't know yet," answered Franklin. "But I want to do something really fun!"

29

Franklin's friends had lots of ideas.
"How about minigolf?" said Snail.
"Or bowling?" suggested Fox.
"Waterslides are fun," said Goose.
"I like squirt tag," said Badger.

Franklin said these were all great ideas.
"But you'll have to choose, Franklin," insisted
Beaver. "We can't do everything."
Franklin thought for a moment.
"We can if we go to Tamarack Play Park,"
he replied. "They have *everything* there!"
Everyone was excited.

Franklin ran home and told his parents the good news. "Tamarack Play Park will be lots of fun," agreed his father. "And I've already invited everyone!" Franklin announced. "Oh dear," said his mother.

Franklin's parents explained the problem.

"Tamarack Play Park is expensive, Franklin," said his father. "We can only take two of your friends."

Franklin felt terrible.

His mother gave him a hug. "I'm sure your other friends will understand."

Franklin wasn't so sure.

Franklin didn't play with his friends for the rest of the day. He stayed in his room and thought about his party. He really wanted to go to Tamarack Play Park. But how could he pick just two of his friends? What would he tell the others?

Franklin sighed. This was *not* going to be the best birthday ever.

At supper that night, Franklin told his parents that he wanted everyone at his party.

"You can have all your friends if your party's in the backyard," his mother suggested.

"But there's so much to do at Tamarack Play Park," said Franklin.

"Too bad we can't bring Tamarack to the backyard!" laughed his father.

Hmm, thought Franklin.

"Maybe we can!" he exclaimed.

Franklin and his parents were busy all that week. They spent lots of time in the toolshed and in the basement and outside in the yard. They made trips to the hardware store and to the party shop.

Franklin didn't tell anyone what they were doing.

35

By noon on Saturday, all of Franklin's friends
had arrived for the party.

"When are we going to Tamarack?" asked Bear.

"Well ... we're not," answered Franklin.

"What do you mean?" demanded Beaver.

Franklin took a deep breath and explained.

"I wanted *all* of you at my party," he finished.
"So ... follow me!"

Franklin led the way to the backyard.

"Welcome to Turtle Play Park," he announced.

"Wow!" said everyone.

All afternoon, Franklin and his friends played minigolf and lawn bowling.

They ran through the sprinkler and slid down the slide into the pond.

They played squirt tag and pin the tail on the turtle.

38

There was lots of food and games and prizes.

Soon it was time for cake and ice cream. Everyone gathered around Franklin and sang "Happy Birthday" with loud and cheerful voices. Afterwards, Franklin opened his gifts, and each one was just right.

When all of his friends had gone home, Franklin thanked his parents.

"Was it the best birthday party ever?" they asked him.

"It sure was," said Franklin.

Then he grinned. "Until next year!"

Activities

Colouring Fun

You're invited to Franklin's birthday party! Draw your gift for Franklin in the box and colour the wrapping.

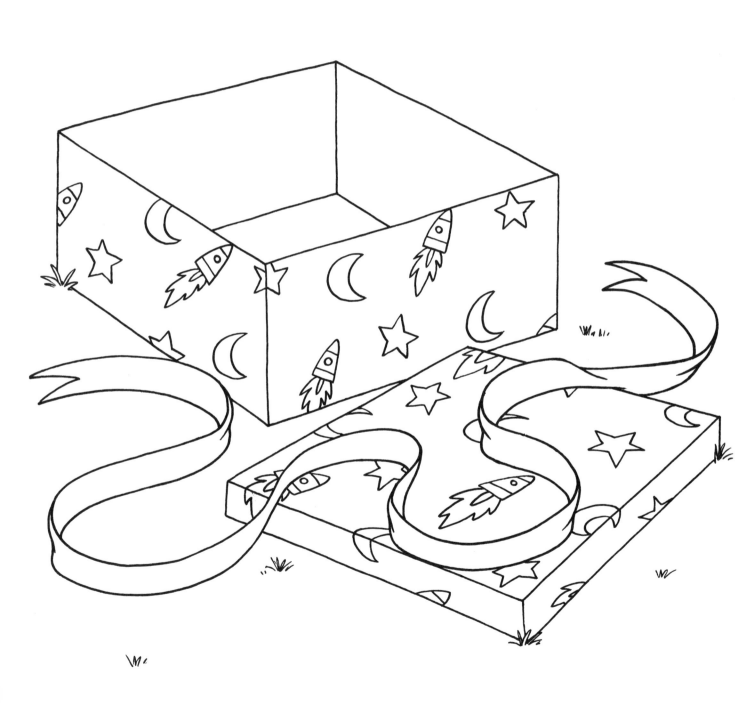

Follow the Ribbon

Oh, no! Snail, Fox and Rabbit have their ribbons all mixed up.
Draw a line along each ribbon to the gift it's attached to.

What's Wrong with This Picture

Everyone has fun playing at Turtle Play Park. But there are many things in this picture that don't belong. Can you find them? Circle each one.

Franklin Runs Away

FRANKLIN could count by twos and tie his shoes. He had lots of good friends and a family who loved him very much. But one day, Franklin couldn't seem to please anybody or do anything right. He decided that no one cared about him at all.

48

It started at breakfast.

Harriet was cranky and fussy. Franklin tried all of his funny faces, but his sister wouldn't smile.

Then Franklin's father said, "I had to put your bicycle away for you last night. That's the third time in three days."

Franklin was told there would be no bike riding for the rest of the week.

At school, Mr. Owl read *Goldilocks and the Three Bears.*

"I wish someone would eat *my* porridge," Franklin whispered to Snail.

"Franklin, this is listening time, not talking time," said Mr. Owl.

Franklin sunk low in his chair.

During recess, Fox complained that Franklin wasn't sharing the ball.

At lunchtime, Beaver changed her mind about trading desserts with Franklin.

On the bus ride home, Bear wanted his book back even though Franklin hadn't finished reading it.

And after school, Badger forgot that she had promised to play with Franklin, and went off with Rabbit instead.

Franklin trudged home. He hoped his mother had made an extra-good snack.

But there wasn't any snack at all.

"I'll be another minute," Franklin's mother called from the garden.

Franklin scowled. He got out bread and butter and jam, and made a big sandwich. When his mother found him, she also found a big mess.

"I'll clean it up," Franklin promised.

"Oh, Franklin!" moaned his mother. "Please just go outside."

Franklin grabbed Sam and some cookies and stomped out the door. He saw Badger and Rabbit flying a kite. He saw Bear heading to the library. He saw Fox and Beaver ride by on their bicycles.

"Nobody likes me," he muttered. "Nobody cares about me at all."

Then Franklin looked at Sam.

"I'm running away!" he declared. "I'm getting a new home and a new school and new friends!"

Franklin bundled up his cookies and marched out of the yard.

Franklin stomped across the bridge and took the path through the meadow. He and his father had gone bicycling this way just the other day.

"Hmmph!" said Franklin. His father would never get to go bike riding with him ever again.

Franklin's tummy began to rumble. He remembered the cookies in his scarf. He had made them yesterday with his mother.

"You're a very big help, Franklin," she had told him.

Well, his mother would never have his help ever again, Franklin thought.

It was late afternoon, and Franklin was tired. He thought about Harriet having her nap. He always played with her as soon as she woke up.

Franklin wondered if Harriet would forget all about him.

Then he remembered how proud she was the first time she said his name.

Franklin sat down to rest. Off in the distance, he could see the park and the soccer field, the pond and the tree house. He thought about his friends having fun, and he wondered if they would miss him.

Then he remembered that his friends had wanted him to be captain of the soccer team.

Soon it would be getting dark. Franklin wondered if his parents would bother to look for him.

Then he remembered the time he was lost. His parents had found him and held him and told him how much they loved him.

57

Franklin looked at the setting sun and thought about eating supper with his family. He thought about finishing his homework and getting another gold star from Mr. Owl. And he thought about the soccer game tomorrow after school.

Franklin sighed a big, deep sigh. He didn't want to find a new home and new friends. He didn't want to find a new teacher.

He wanted the family who loved him and the friends who played with him and the teacher who taught him interesting things.

Franklin ran all the way back.

When he got to his yard, he saw Harriet at the window and he could smell supper on the table. His father was at the door, calling his name.

"Here I am," Franklin answered. "I'm home!"

Activities

Going Home Maze

Franklin wants to go home. Help him get there as quickly as possible.

START

FINISH

Connect the Dots

When Franklin gets home, someone gives him a great big hug. Connect the dots to find out who it is.

Word Search

Franklin finds out there are lots of reasons not to run away. In the puzzle below, circle words from the story. You'll find the words going up, down, across and diagonally.

```
H  E  M  O  T  H  E  R  J  A
O  L  G  I  W  L  I  G  O  H
M  T  E  A  C  H  E  R  X  S
E  P  M  Y  N  A  U  H  D  O
O  F  C  L  P  R  I  N  K  C
A  I  C  I  E  R  E  W  A  C
B  P  V  M  O  I  G  K  S  E
J  L  N  A  R  E  G  U  B  R
P  E  K  F  A  T  H  E  R  N
U  H  Q  E  R  Y  J  L  D  Z
```

BICYCLE   TEACHER

FAMILY   MOTHER

FATHER   SOCCER

FRIENDS   HOME

HARRIET   HELP

Word Scramble

Fill in the blanks by unscrambling the letters in each box.

1. Harriet won't smile, so Franklin tries all his funny
___ ___ ___ ___ ___ . | a s c f e |

2. During story time, Mr. Owl catches Franklin
___ ___ ___ ___ ___ ___ ___ . | l a k i t n g |

3. Fox wants Franklin to share the ___ ___ ___ ___ . | l a l b |

4. Instead of playing with Franklin, Badger goes off with
___ ___ ___ ___ ___ ___ . | b t i b R a |

5. When Franklin runs away, he takes some cookies and
___ ___ ___ . | m S a |

6. Franklin's mother always tells him he's a big help when
they make ___ ___ ___ ___ ___ ___ ___ . | k o o i c s e |

Franklin and the Babysitter

FRANKLIN could count by twos and tie his shoes. He was old enough to walk to Bear's house alone and go to the ice cream store on his own. But Franklin wasn't old enough to stay home all by himself. When his parents went out, Granny came to take care of him.

One afternoon, Franklin's parents were getting ready to go to a party. Franklin and Harriet were watching out the window.

"When's Granny going to get here?" Franklin asked. "I want to show her my new puzzle. And she promised to bring her fudge."

Just then the phone rang, and there was bad news. Granny was sick with a cold.

Franklin was very disappointed. So was his mother.

"I really wanted to go to that party," she sighed.

"We can still go," said Franklin's father. "We'll get a babysitter."

"I don't want a babysitter," complained Franklin. "I want Granny."

"Granny is a babysitter," replied his father.

"No, she isn't," answered Franklin. "Granny's Granny."

Franklin's mother started making phone calls. Soon she announced that Mrs. Muskrat could babysit.

"Mrs. Muskrat?!" cried Franklin. "But she's never taken care of us before. She won't know what to do. She —"

"Franklin," replied his father. "You and Harriet like Mrs. Muskrat. You'll have fun together."

"Hmph!" said Franklin.

Mrs. Muskrat arrived at five o'clock and settled in.

"If you need anything, here's the phone number," said Franklin's mother.

"Don't worry about us," said Mrs. Muskrat, shooing Franklin's parents out the door. "We'll be just fine. Won't we, Franklin?"

Franklin wasn't so sure.

Mrs. Muskrat turned to Franklin and Harriet.
"Why don't you two keep me company while
I start supper?"

"Can we do my puzzle?" Franklin asked.

"First thing after I make us a nice soup,"
replied Mrs. Muskrat.

Franklin frowned.

"Granny does puzzles first thing," he said.

73

It wasn't long before Mrs. Muskrat called
Franklin and Harriet to the table. Franklin peered
into his soup bowl.

"Are those brussels sprouts? I hate brussels
sprouts!" he exclaimed.

"I'm sorry, Franklin," said Mrs. Muskrat. "I
didn't know."

"Granny knows," Franklin muttered.

When supper was finished, Mrs. Muskrat asked
Franklin and Harriet what they would like for dessert.

"Granny always brings fudge," replied Franklin.

"Well, why don't we make some?" suggested
Mrs. Muskrat.

Franklin got out sugar and butter and cocoa.
Harriet got out pots and pans. Franklin cheered
up a bit as the sweet smell filled the air.

As soon as the fudge was ready, Mrs. Muskrat gave Franklin the first piece.

"Is it good?" she asked.

Franklin nodded. "But Granny always puts flies in her fudge," he said.

"Oh dear," sighed Mrs. Muskrat. "I forgot how much you love flies."

"Granny never forgets," said Franklin.

As Mrs. Muskrat was cleaning up the kitchen, Franklin turned on the radio.

"Welcome to *Shadow Land*," said the announcer.

Mrs. Muskrat frowned.

"I think that show is a little too scary for a young turtle," she said.

"No, it isn't," declared Franklin.

Then he fibbed. "*Granny* lets me listen."

Mrs. Muskrat sighed.

Mrs. Muskrat left to put Harriet to bed. Franklin settled into his chair.

The show began with moans and sighs and eerie cries. Then came clanking and creaking, rustling and squeaking. Franklin looked about him. What was that shadow beside his bedroom door? What was that tapping noise in the corner?

Mrs. Muskrat found Franklin shivering and shaking in his chair. She turned off the radio and held him on her lap.

"I'm sorry, Mrs. Muskrat," Franklin whimpered. "Granny doesn't let me listen to *Shadow Land*. Now I'm too scared to go to sleep."

Franklin started to cry.

Mrs. Muskrat thought for a moment. Then she said, "If I were Granny, I'd let you stay up late and keep me company."

Franklin wiped his eyes.

"I think Granny would do that," he agreed.

When his parents came home, Franklin and Mrs. Muskrat were sipping hot chocolate in front of a glowing fire. They were on their second bowl of popcorn and their third puzzle.

As Mrs. Muskrat was leaving, Franklin gave her a big hug.

"Granny's still my Granny," he told her. "But you're my favourite babysitter."

Activities

Connect the Dots

Who is Franklin's favourite babysitter? Connect the dots to find out.

Spot the Difference

Circle the picture in each row that is different from the others.

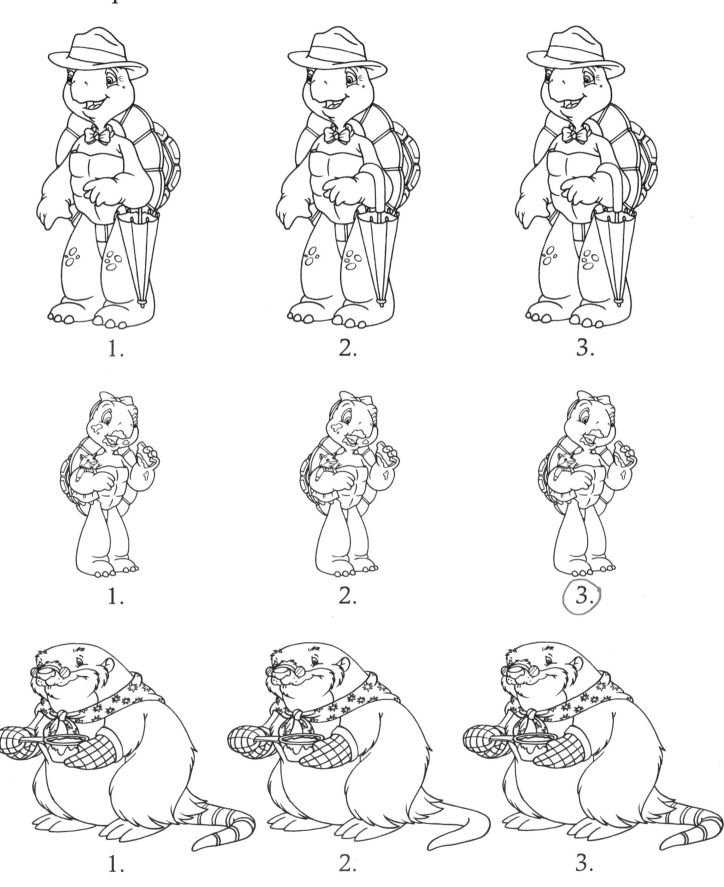

1.

2.

3.

1.

2.

3.

1.

2.

3.

Search and Find

Franklin wants to work on his puzzle, but some of the pieces are missing. Can you help him find the them? Circle each one.

I found _13_ puzzle pieces.

Answers

Word Scramble – p. 22
1. wagon   4. chart
2. maple   5. red
3. swing   6. Heron

Tree Maze – p. 23

Spot the Difference – p. 25
Franklin – #3
Tree – #1
Rabbit – #2

Going Home Maze – p. 62

Word Scramble – p. 65
1. faces   4. Rabbit
2. talking   5. Sam
3. ball   6. cookies

Spot the Difference – p. 85
Dad – #1
Harriet – #3
Mrs. Muskrat – #2

Search and Find – p. 86–87
There are 23 puzzle pieces.

What's Wrong with This Picture – pp. 44–45

pail on Fox's head
baseball bat
sock on minigolf pole
Bear's hockey helmet
jack-o-lantern balloon
cake on slide
lollipop on cattail
soccer ball
teacup on lily pad
candles in grass
Rabbit's baseball glove
golf flag on cattail
Franklin's bicycle helmet

piece of cake on
   lily pad
hockey stick
bed
Badger's elbow pad
Goose's sock
carrots on bush
snowman
present in tree
mitten on flowers
lamp
vase
Skunk's hockey skate

Word Search – p. 24

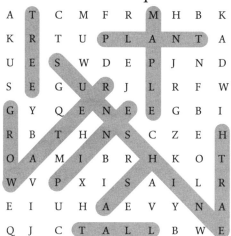

Word Search – p. 64

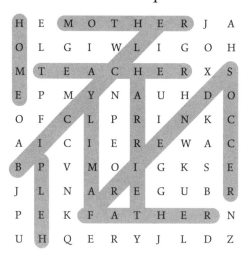

88